Dear Parent:
Your child's love of reading starts here!

Every child learns to read in a different way and at his or her own speed. Some go back and forth between reading levels and read favorite books again and again. Others read through each level in order. You can help your young reader improve and become more confident by encouraging his or her own interests and abilities. From books your child reads with you to the first books he or she reads alone, there are I Can Read Books for every stage of reading:

SHARED READING
Basic language, word repetition, and whimsical illustrations, ideal for sharing with your emergent reader

BEGINNING READING
Short sentences, familiar words, and simple concepts for children eager to read on their own

READING WITH HELP
Engaging stories, longer sentences, and language play for developing readers

READING ALONE
Complex plots, challenging vocabulary, and high-interest topics for the independent reader

ADVANCED READING
Short paragraphs, chapters, and exciting themes for the perfect bridge to chapter books

I Can Read Books have introduced children to the joy of reading since 1957. Featuring award-winning authors and illustrators and a fabulous cast of beloved characters, I Can Read Books set the standard for beginning readers.

A lifetime of discovery begins with the magical words "I Can Read!"

Visit www.icanread.com for information
on enriching your child's reading experience.

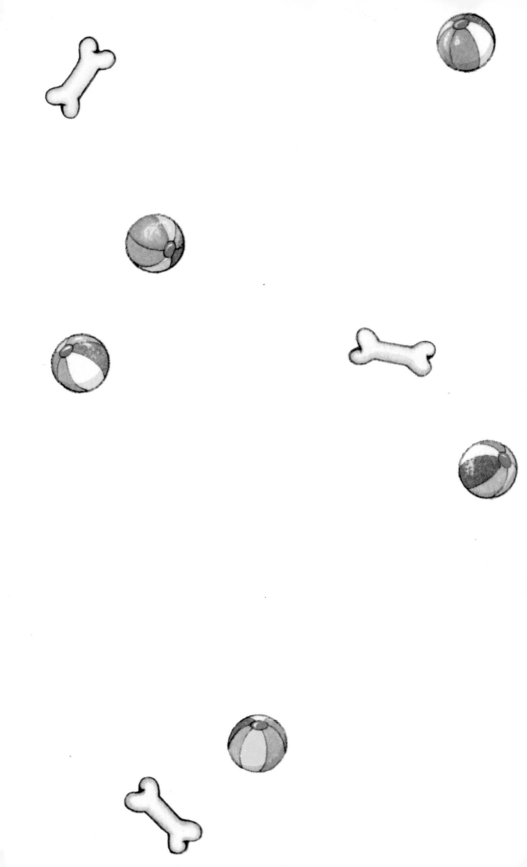

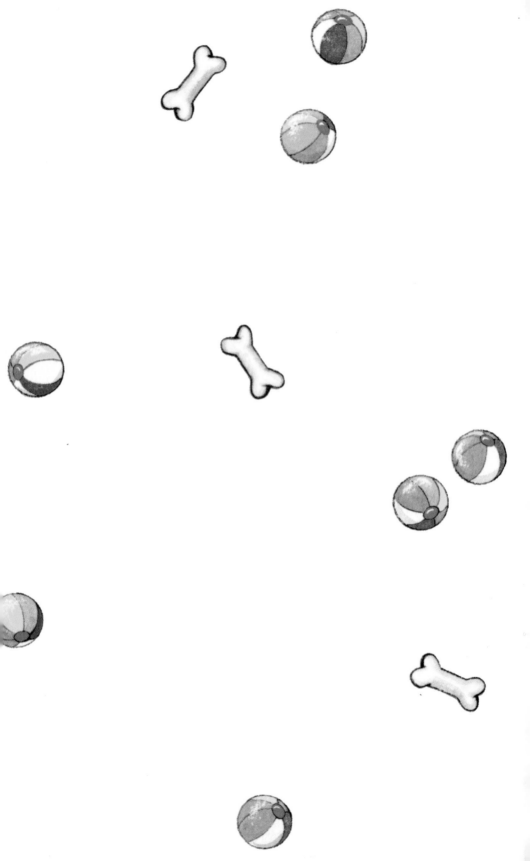

For Peter and
Laura
—A.S.C.

HarperCollins®, ✎®, and I Can Read Book® are trademarks of HarperCollins Publishers.

Library of Congress Cataloging-in-Publication Data
Capucilli, Alyssa Satin.
  Biscuit and the little pup / story by Alyssa Satin Capucilli ; pictures by Pat Schories.— 1st ed.
    p.   cm.—(I can read book)
  ISBN 978-06-074170-9 (trade bdg.) — ISBN 978-0-06-074171-6 (lib. bdg.) — ISBN 978-0-06-074172-3 (pbk.)
  [1. Dogs—Fiction. 2. Animals—Infancy—Fiction. 3. Play—Fiction.] I. Schories, Pat, ill. II. Title.
PZ7.C179Big 2008   2007006994
[E-—22   CIP
                                                                                                             AC
──
          14 15 16 17 18 LP/WOR 10 9   ❖   First Edition

I Can Read!™

SHARED READING

My First

Biscuit and the Little Pup

story by ALYSSA SATIN CAPUCILLI
pictures by PAT SCHORIES

HarperCollins*Publishers*

Here, Biscuit.

It's time to play.

Woof, woof!

You found your ball, Biscuit.

Arf!

You found a little pup, too.

Woof, woof!

Come out, little pup.

What is your name?

Woof, woof!

Come out, little pup.

Biscuit wants to play!

Woof, woof!

Arf!

The little pup does not want

to come out.

Here, little pup.

Biscuit has a ball.

Woof, woof!

Biscuit has a bone.

Woof, woof!

Won't you come out,
little pup?

Arf! Arf!
The little pup does not want
to come out yet.

What will we do now?

Woof!

Wait, Biscuit.

Where are you going?

Woof, woof!
Silly puppy!
It's not time for you to hide.

Arf! Arf! Arf! Arf!

Woof, woof!

Oh, Biscuit!

Here comes the little pup!

Woof, woof!

Arf! Arf!

Funny puppies!

You both want to play.

You want to play
hide-and-seek!

Woof, woof!

Ready or not, sweet puppies,

we found both of you!

Arf! Arf!

Woof!

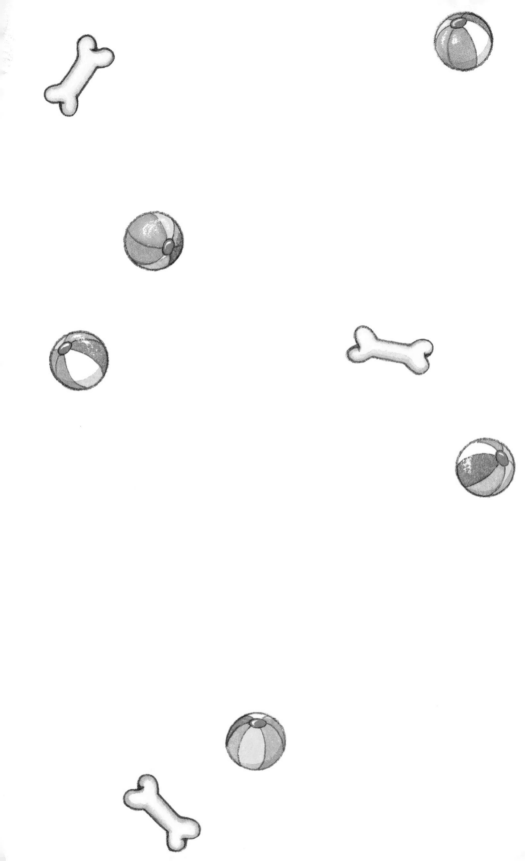

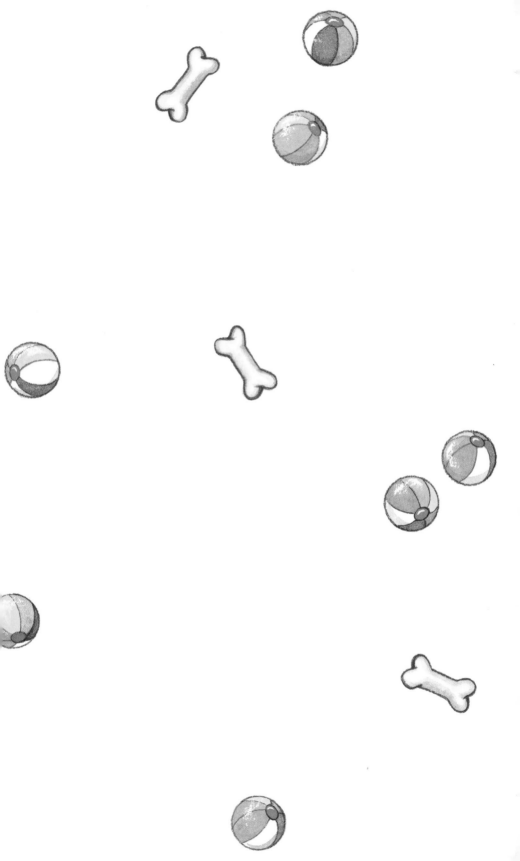